After
the
Snowfall

Rich Lo

Guilford, Connecticut

Dedicated to my parents, who kept our family together through tough times in a country and culture they knew very little about.

An imprint of The Rowman & Littlefield Publishing Group, Inc.
4501 Forbes Blvd., Ste. 200
Lanham, MD 20706
www.rowman.com

MuddyBootsBooks.com

Distributed by NATIONAL BOOK NETWORK

British Library Cataloguing in Publication Information available

Library of Congress Control Number: 2020942902

ISBN 978-1-63076-390-9 (hardcover : alk. paper)
ISBN 978-1-63076-391-6 (electronic)

Printed in Dongguan, PRC, China
September 2020

A fox peeks out of his den at a white forest.

All is silent.

A buck stands
hidden by the trees.

A great horned owl sits on a nearby branch.

The fox climbs
out of his den.

He stops to watch
squirrels eat.

He passes mice foraging
for seeds beneath the snow.

The fox reaches a stream where he takes a cold drink.

A family of mallard ducks swims by.

Across the stream,
river otters rest on a rock.

Suddenly the earth trembles.

The fox walks quietly
past the moose.

His thirst
quenched,
the fox
heads home.

He passes rabbits hiding
in a hollow log.

Chattering crows greet
the fox outside his den.

After the
snowfall.

Rich Lo

Rich Lo is an award-winning author/illustrator and a commercial and fine artist. His work can be found on packaging and ads for national brands and on large installations in public buildings. His first picture book, *Father's Chinese Opera*, was named an ALA Asian/Pacific American Award for Literature Honor book. A combination of imagination and technical excellence characterizes Rich's style.